Chapter 1

Clare was lonely. That afternoon, she'd put away her toys in cupboards and her books on shelves in her new room. She'd played with Tommy while Mum and Dad arranged furniture and unpacked pots and pans. Now they were cooking their first meal in the new kitchen in the new house.

It was spaghetti bolognese, and she'd been hoping for fish and chips. She wrinkled her nose and kicked her trainer against the skirting-board.

"Don't do that," said Dad, stirring the bolognese sauce.

"Go and play with Tommy," said Mum.

"He's gone to sleep," said Clare. She'd played with Tommy all day, and it was a relief when he'd fallen asleep in the play-pen, sucking his thumb, with his bottom in the air.

"Oh dear," said Mum. "You shouldn't have let him go to sleep. Now he probably won't sleep tonight."

"I couldn't help it," said Clare.

The cat with two lives

ELEANOR WATKINS

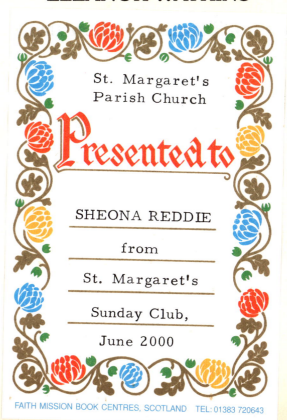

St. Margaret's
Parish Church

Presented to

SHEONA REDDIE

from

St. Margaret's

Sunday Club,

June 2000

To Thomas and Snoopy

By the same author

Nobody's Dog (Read by Myself)
The Vicarage Rats (Tiger)

© Eleanor Watkins 1999
First published 1999

ISBN 1 85999 295 1

British Library Cataloguing-in-Publication Data.
A catalogue record for this book is available from the British Library.

Printed and bound in Great Britain by Creative Print and Design (Wales), Ebbw Vale.

"Well, never mind," said Mum. "Whatever's the matter, Clare? You do sound cross."

Clare thought they all sounded cross. Mum's hair was flopping over her face and she kept pushing it back. Dad looked tired and was frowning a bit. Moving was hard work.

"I'm lonely," said Clare. Her mouth turned down at the corners. "I wish I had a friend."

"Well, you will have," said Mum briskly, fishing cutlery from a crate. "Heaps of friends, I expect, when you go to school and get to know people."

"They might not like me," said Clare. The thought of going to a new school, with new people, gave her a hollow feeling in her stomach. She kicked the skirting-board again. Then she noticed something she hadn't seen before. In the bottom of the blue-painted back door, there was another door. A tiny door that hung downwards on hinges. She pushed it with her foot and it swung to and fro, squeaking a little.

"What's this little door for?" asked Clare.

"That's a cat flap," said Dad. "So that a cat can get in and out by itself."

Clare thought that was a lovely idea. "Could we get a cat?"

But Dad shook his head. "We're not all that keen on cats. I'll probably take out the cat flap and fill in the gap."

"I'm keen on cats," said Clare. "Why can't I have one?"

"You're getting quite whiny," said Mum. "Come and put out the table mats. You'll feel better after a good meal."

"I feel all right now," said Clare. "Just lonely."

They served up the spaghetti bolognese and sat down at the table. Dad said thank you to God for moving safely to the new house. Mum glanced at Clare and asked that God would soon give her a new friend so that she wouldn't be lonely. They all said thank you for the food. "But I wish we had some pudding as well," added Clare.

"You'll have to fill up with biscuits," said Mum. "If I can find the biscuit tin."

They all enjoyed the spaghetti. They were just finishing when a knock came at the door. Mum went to answer it. Clare could see a blonde woman standing there with a tray. She and Mum talked and laughed for a few minutes. Then Mum came in with the tray.

"That was someone from the church. Pat Heslop, I think she said. She knew we were moving in today and thought we'd like some tea and cheesecake. Wasn't that nice?" She glanced at Clare and added ,"She's got a daughter your age, Clare. She's called Katie. She thought you might like to go round to play."

Dad divided up the cheesecake while Mum poured tea from the big brown pot. "Well," she said. "Seems you've got someone to be a new friend."

She and Dad looked at each other, suddenly happy and sparkling as though they felt that everything was going to be all right. Clare wasn't so sure. The pudding was lovely: creamy and fruity to the last spoonful. But she didn't know what to think about the new friend.

"What if I don't like her? What if she doesn't like me?"

Mum laughed and gave her a big hug. "Don't worry! Everything's working out fine. Let's go and wake Tommy and get him bathed and fed."

Tommy hated being woken from a nap and cried very loudly. When things had quietened down a little, Clare remembered the cat flap. She looked at it when Mum sent her to the kitchen with Tommy's plastic cup and dish. She nudged the cat flap with her toe and it squeaked.

"I wish I had a cat," she said under her breath. Suddenly she remembered her prayers for a friend, and how God had answered.

She still had a few doubts about the friend, but she prayed, "God, could you send me a cat?"

She didn't really think that this prayer would be answered too, but there was no harm in asking. A little while later, when Mum and Dad were watching TV, she went to fetch a drink before bed. Suddenly the cat flap swung open and a big, black cat came walking through.

Chapter 2

The cat looked at Clare, and Clare looked at the cat. The cat seemed rather surprised to see her. It stood with one front paw lifted, and its tail curled like a question mark. Its eyes were very large, with little dark flecks in the middle of them. It had shiny black fur, with just a bit of white on its paws and on its face. It was very large, and Clare thought it was the most beautiful cat she had ever seen.

"Clare!" called Mum from the sitting room. "Hurry up! Bedtime!"

Clare held her breath, hoping that the cat would not be frightened and turn round and go away again. But it didn't. It stared at her for a moment or two longer, then it said, "Trooo?" in a questioning kind of way as though it was asking her name. Then it stalked over to the fridge and sat down beside it and said, "Trooo?" again.

"Do you want some milk?" asked Clare.

"Clare!" called Mum again. "Did you say something?"

Clare thought that she'd better answer, or they'd come bursting in and frighten the cat. She went and stood in the doorway.

"Is something the matter?" asked Mum.

"A cat came in," said Clare.

At first they thought she was making up stories. But they had to believe her when they came into the kitchen themselves and saw the cat sitting there by the fridge door.

"That's the worst thing about cat flaps," said Dad. "All the strays in the neighbourhood can come in."

"It doesn't look like a stray," said Mum. "It looks very well cared for. And well fed. I wonder who it belongs to?"

"It doesn't belong to anyone," said Clare. "Just before it came, I asked God if we could have a cat. And then this one came. It's ours."

Mum and Dad looked at each other. They had the kind of look that meant they were thinking very carefully what to say. Dad cleared his throat and said, "We can't be sure about that. I think this cat must belong to someone. Prayers aren't always answered just like that, straight away."

"That's not what you said before," said Clare, "about a friend for me."

Mum and Dad looked at each other again. Mum said, "All the same, I think we'd better make enquiries about this cat tomorrow. It's a very nice cat. Maybe it would like some milk."

"It would," said Clare quickly.

"That's encouraging it," said Dad. "It'll think it can come in and get fed all the time."

But Clare and her mum won. While Mum got out a carton of milk and Clare fetched a saucer, the cat jumped up and twined itself about their legs, purring loudly. It lapped up all the milk, then sat down to clean its paws and whiskers.

"It certainly seems to feel at home," said Mum.

"Well, it had better not get too comfortable," said Dad.

Clare didn't say anything. She squeezed her hands very tightly together and hoped very hard that they could keep the cat.

Afterwards, Dad insisted that the cat be put outside the door. Clare couldn't bear to think of it out there in the dark alone.

They went to bed for the first time in the new house. It had been a long tiring day, and they all slept soundly.

Clare was up early, before anyone else, even Tommy. In her pyjamas she tiptoed downstairs to the kitchen. Packing cases lay about, with lots of things inside still waiting to be unpacked. One of them was full of bedding, spare duvets and winter blankets and extra pillows. On the top of it, curled up on a blue cot cover, the black cat lay peacefully asleep.

"That cat will have to go," said Dad at breakfast time. "It can't just move in on us like that."

The cat seemed to think it had already moved in. It sat by the fridge until they gave it a saucer of porridge and milk. Then it sat by the stove and purred while it cleaned its whiskers. It liked Clare to stroke it. Tommy loved the cat. He leaned sideways from his high chair, offering spoonfuls of porridge to the cat.

He chortled when they dripped onto the floor and the cat came and licked them up. Clare knew that Mum liked the cat too, although she didn't admit it in front of Dad. She said, "We'll go to the shops this morning. On the way, I'll enquire among the neighbours. We'll see if they know who it belongs to."

Dad was going to the DIY store, so he dropped them off at the supermarket. When they left, the cat was outside, asleep in the sun on the garden wall. They arrived home laden with supermarket bags hooked onto Tommy's buggy.

"I'll try next door before we go in," said Mum.

A plump middle-aged lady answered her knock. "Lovely to meet you," she said, shaking hands and beaming. "I do hope you'll be happy here. A black cat? Oh yes, that'll be old Oliver. He was the Brownlows' cat. Those were the people who lived in your house before."

"But didn't they take him with them?"

asked Mum.

The lady wrinkled her forehead. "I'm not really sure. They both worked and I didn't see that much of them. Maybe they did take him, and he came back. Cats do that sometimes, you know. He was always a bit of a roamer, was Oliver. Came and went to suit himself. Cats are like that."

Clare was jumping from one foot to the other. Did this mean that they could keep Oliver? She couldn't wait to get home and see him again.

Oliver wasn't there when they let themselves in.

"Do you think he'll come back?" she asked anxiously.

"I expect so," said Mum. "You heard what the lady next door said."

"And can we keep him?" asked Clare.

Mum lifted Tommy out of the buggy. "If he's not claimed, then, yes, I think we can. It sounds as though he never left here really."

"But what will Dad say?"

Mum smiled. "You leave Dad to me. I think he'll come round. I think it'll be all right."

Clare gave a skip of joy. If Mum believed it, it would be all right. And Mum must believe it, because she'd bought about twelve tins of cat food along with the other groceries.

Chapter 3

There were so many new things to get used to: a new home in a new neighbourhood, new shops and new neighbours.

There was a new job for Dad and they had a new pet, because Oliver did come back again that evening, popping in through the cat flap with a loud "Trooo!" of greeting.

He sat by the fridge until he was fed, and after he had washed himself he went into the sitting-room and settled down in front of the fire.

"That cat thinks he owns the place!" grumbled Dad.

But in spite of the grumbles, Dad didn't make Clare put Oliver out that evening. There was no more mention of stopping up the cat flap. Mum had explained the situation, and she and Clare thought that it was going to be all right.

"I do believe we've got ourselves a cat!" said Mum, when she tucked Clare into bed. "Yes!" said Clare, and she and Mum slapped their hands together.

On Monday, there would be a new school, but before that, there was the new church.

The first person Clare saw when they went into church on Sunday morning was the blonde lady who'd brought them the tea and cheesecake. She turned and gave them a little wave and a big smile. She was sitting with a tall man and some tall young people. Squashed in between them was a girl who Clare thought must be the one who was supposed to be her new friend. She noticed that the girl had dark curly hair with a red hairband, and she was wearing a blue jacket with a hood. She frowned a bit and fidgeted, because there wasn't much room in the seat with all the big people.

There was Children's Church half-way through, and the other children went out of the main room into a smaller one. A lady asked if Clare wanted to go too, but suddenly she didn't want to. Everything was strange and there was not one face that she knew. It was all too new. The lady smiled and said, "Never mind!" Clare stayed with Mum and Dad and Tommy for the rest of the service.

"I'm afraid she's a bit shy," Mum told people afterwards.

"How about coming to play with Katie one day?" asked the blonde lady. "She often gets lonely because the others are so much older."

But Clare felt more shy than ever when she saw all of Katie's brothers and sisters, looking down at her and smiling.

"Maybe Katie could come to our house first," suggested Mum.

"Good idea!" said Katie's mum. Clare squirmed. She wasn't at all sure that she wanted to play with Katie after all. She wished she hadn't complained so much about being lonely and needing a friend. She had Oliver now, and he was cuddly and warm and always pleased to see her. She felt he was the only friend she needed.

But the two mums were busy making plans, taking no notice of her. "Maybe this afternoon," said Clare's mum. Katie's mum replied, "Good idea! Then they'll have a chance to get to know each other before school starts."

That very afternoon Katie was brought by car and left on the doorstep by her oldest brother.

She bustled in and looked around. Her face was round and rosy and her dark curls bounced. When they stood together, Clare found that Katie was quite a bit taller than herself. Katie was not at all shy either.

"Could I see your room?" she asked, after she had said "hello" and taken off her coat.

Clare led the way upstairs. Katie looked around at everything, with bright dark eyes. Then she looked at Clare.

"How old are you?"

"Seven and a half," said Clare.

"I'm much older. I'll be eight soon," said Katie importantly. "My bedroom is much bigger than this. It's got three beds. One for me, one for my sister Bridget and one for my sister Emily. They both go to the High School. Do you have any sisters?"

Clare shook her head. Katie's eyes gleamed. "I've got two big brothers as well. Sam and Robert. Robert can drive a car. He drove me here this afternoon."

Clare was impressed. Fancy having a brother grown up enough to drive a car! She wished she had bigger brothers and sisters. She said, "I've got a brother."

"Have you?" said Katie. She twirled in front of the mirror. "How long is your hair? Let's see whose is longest."

Clare didn't really like being ordered about. But they took off their hairbands and measured hair. As she'd expected, Katie's was the longest, and thickest and curliest. Katie looked round the room again.

"Haven't you got a TV?"

"It's downstairs," said Clare.

"Me and Bridget and Emily have our own." Katie told her. "Well, let's go down and watch cartoons then."

Mum switched on the TV for them while she and Dad got tea ready in the kitchen.

Tommy was playing in the sitting-room. "Is that your brother?" asked Katie. Clare nodded. Tommy was teething and

dribbling down his chin. One cheek was redder than the other and his nose was running a bit because he had a cold coming. Katie stared at him and Clare thought she shuddered. Clare got a tissue and mopped up Tommy's nose and chin.

"We've got a dog," said Katie. "He's called Max. He's a Labrador. I've got a hamster too. And a rabbit."

Clare felt envious. She'd always wished she could keep pets. Then she remembered Oliver. "We've got a cat," she said. "A black one. Really big. As big as that." She held her two hands a good distance apart.

"We've got a cat too," said Katie quickly. "This big."

She held her hands even further apart, and added, "Where's your cat, then?"

Clare went to look, but Oliver wasn't in the kitchen or the garden. He'd gone wandering off again.

"He's not in at the moment," she told Katie.

Katie looked as though she didn't believe that Clare had a cat at all. Clare sat down again, further away from Katie on the sofa. She wished tea was ready. She wished it was time for Katie to go home. She wished her mum hadn't made her be friends with such a bossy person. She almost wished they hadn't moved here at all.

Chapter 4

School was not as bad as Clare thought it might be. She had a nice teacher called Miss Simmonds, who made sure that Clare felt at home in the new class.

"I don't expect you know anyone," she said when Mum had left her in the classroom, "so I'll ask Sarah and Emma if they'll show you the way round today."

She called Sarah and Emma over and introduced them. Sarah had blonde hair in bunches and Emma had two front teeth missing. Clare thought they both looked nice. They were showing Clare where to hang up her coat and shoebag, when Katie came bursting into the cloakroom. Her eyes were sparkling and her cheeks glowing.

"Oh, hello, Clare! Don't worry, I'll take care of you." She turned to Sarah and Emma. "Clare's my friend. I'll show her everything. These are the toilets, Clare. And that's where we wash our hands. And along the corridor there is where we go to have lunch."

She took Clare's hand and led her firmly around. Sarah and Emma looked at each other and then went off by themselves. Clare was rather sorry. She'd liked the look of them.

Katie took care of her all day long, sitting next to her in class, taking her to dinner, even telling her what things to eat. "Better have the cottage pie. That's what I'm having."

Clare would have preferred the cauliflower cheese. It looked nice and golden and bubbly. But before she knew it, she was sitting opposite Katie at a table, with a plate of cottage pie in front of her.

Katie showed Clare where to change for PE, and told her which book to take out of the library. But at least Clare never felt lonely or left out all day, not once.

"How was school?" asked Mum, when she and Tommy came to meet Clare in the afternoon.

"All right," said Clare. She thought school was going to be fine, though she felt quite worn out after that first day. It was a relief to be home, with just Mum getting her a drink, and Tommy dribbling and playing with his toy cars.

"It must have been a great help, having Katie there," said Mum.

"Yes," said Clare.

"Good!" said Mum. "I'm glad you're becoming good friends. Her mum has asked you for tea after school tomorrow."

Clare's heart sank. Katie had a whole big family. She wished she didn't have to meet a lot more people just yet. She just needed Mum and Dad and Tommy, after school, until she was more used to everything, and Oliver.

"Where's Oliver?" she asked.

Mum handed her a glass of juice. "He was here when we left this morning. But he had gone when I got back from the shops. He'll be back. You know what he's like."

Just then Oliver came in through the cat flap, looking very plump and sleek and very pleased to see Clare. He walked up to her and said "Trooo?" and butted his head against her. Clare thought he was asking where she'd been all day.

"I've been at school," she told him. "My new school. Where have you been?"

But Oliver wasn't saying any more. He wound himself around Clare's legs, and while she drank her juice he had a saucer of milk.

Afterwards they watched TV together, curled up on the sofa. Oliver purred so loudly that his body rumbled and his whiskers quivered. He was warm and comforting. Clare was so glad she had Oliver. She couldn't think how she had ever managed without him. It didn't matter if things were new and strange, and if Katie was a bit too bossy. At least she had Oliver.

When Mum came in a little later, Clare and Oliver were both sound asleep.

Katie's mum picked them both up from school next day. Katie's house was large and it stood in a big garden, with trees and shrubs and outhouses. A huge black Labrador waited for them in the driveway.

"Max," said Katie. "Come and say hello!"

Max seemed very large but Katie's mum said he was a real old softie. He waved his tail and tried to lick Clare's face with a long slobbery tongue. Katie took Clare to the outhouses to see the rest of her pets. There was a rabbit called Mopsy, with long ears that flopped over instead of standing up. And there was a hamster called Hamish, who stuffed food into his cheek pouches until they bulged out at each side of his face.

They looked about for Katie's cat Thomas
but he was not to be found.

"He does wander off," said Katie.

"Cats are like that," said Clare.

Katie's house was bright and untidy
inside. It seemed big and empty with just
Clare and Katie and Katie's mum. Then
Katie's brothers and sisters began to arrive
home from the High School and college,
and it suddenly seemed full of people, all
laughing and talking and shouting.

"Hello, Clare," said Bridget, the eldest girl. She was dark-haired like Katie. "Nice to see you. Katie, go upstairs and get my trainers, will you? I'm off to aerobics."

"And fetch my blue top while you're at it," said Emily, who was blonde. "I need to iron it."

Katie and Clare went upstairs together. The girls' room was large and cluttered. Clothes, books, bags, shoes, magazines and CDs were littered around on beds and chairs and on the floor. Katie rummaged around for the trainers and blue top.

On the way down, they met Sam, who was leaping upstairs two at a time on his long legs. He grinned at them, and said, "Oh, Katie – have a look for my red towel, will you? I need it for football practice."

Robert, the brother who drove a car, left his keys upstairs and sent Katie back up to fetch them. Clare's legs began to feel very tired from going up and down stairs with Katie, fetching and carrying.

Loud music played and the big people laughed and shouted and slammed doors and took showers. One or other of them was on the phone the whole time. Often they'd think of something they should remember to do, and asked Katie to do it for them. Katie always did. Clare began to feel quite sorry for her. It was a relief when some of them went out again, and the two girls could sit down and have their tea in peace.

"Did you enjoy meeting Katie's family?" Dad asked later.

"I think so," said Clare. "They're nice. But there's such a lot of them. And they're big. And bossy."

"As bossy as Katie?" asked Mum.

"Much bossier," said Clare.

Chapter 5

Everyone was settling nicely. Dad liked his new job; Clare was settling into her new school. All of them were settling into their new home and new church. Oliver was settling nicely too, coming and going as he pleased, but always returning to eat enormous meals and curl up, purring loudly, next to Clare. His favourite food seemed to be kippers, and he always managed to be on time if there were kippers for tea.

Another week had passed, and Katie was coming to play and to spend the night.

"It's called sleeping over," she told Clare.

"My sisters do it all the time."

Clare wasn't quite sure that she wanted Katie to sleep over. But she was glad that she'd have a chance to show Oliver to Katie. He was so beautiful, so black and sleek and shiny. Katie was sure to admire him.

Oliver came into the bedroom before school when she and Mum were getting ready for Katie's visit. He sat on the window sill in the morning sun, washing himself and pretending to take no notice. But all the time he was keeping one eye on what they were doing.

Mum put up a little folding bed for Katie and found a nice plump pillow and a sky-blue duvet.

"What about the lamp?" asked Mum.

Clare had a little lamp with a dim bulb in her bedroom as well as the main light. Sometimes, she kept it on all night. There were times when she felt a little worried – not scared exactly, just worried. The little bit of light made all the difference.

Clare thought Katie might think the lamp was babyish. She was sure Katie never needed a light at night, not even one with a dim bulb.

"I don't think I'll need the lamp," she told Mum.

Katie came home from school with Clare, and Katie began to decide what they'd do right from the start. She chose what they had for tea, and she chose the video they would watch afterwards. She decided that they would go to bed early.

"But I wanted to show you Oliver," said Clare.

"Well, where is he then?" asked Katie.

Oliver had taken himself off just before home time, Mum said, and he hadn't turned up again yet. Clare felt quite cross with him. She wanted so much to show him off to Katie. But Katie wasn't going to wait up for him. Clare sometimes had the feeling that Katie didn't really believe she had a cat at all.

They had their baths and bedtime drinks, and Mum tucked them up with a story and prayers. Clare had been right about the lamp. She found she didn't need it at all, with Katie there in the other bed. It was getting dark, but she could just see Katie's hands gripping the top of the duvet.

"Clare?" said Katie's voice from the other bed.

Clare jumped awake. "Yes?"

"Nothing. I just wanted to see if you were still awake." She paused, and then went on, "At home, I share with Bridget and Emily. They're bigger than me."

"I know," said Clare. "They're at the High School."

She thought Katie's voice sounded smaller than usual somehow. She hoped Oliver would be back by morning. Her eyes were closing.

Katie gave a sudden shriek. "Oh! Could you put the light on? I think there's a spider on my bed!"

Clare switched on the lamp and climbed out of bed. They couldn't find any spider, so they decided that the spider must have been a loose bit of thread dangling from the blue duvet cover.

"Are you going to switch off the light?" asked Katie.

Clare had been going to, but suddenly she felt that Katie didn't want the light to go off. She pulled her own duvet up under her chin.

"No," she said. "Sometimes I leave it on all night. Sometimes I get a bit worried at night, and then I leave it on."

"All right," said Katie. "I don't mind. If you're worried." She paused, and then she said, "Are you a bit worried because Oliver hasn't come back?"

Clare wasn't really worried about Oliver, because he always came back. But she was disappointed that she hadn't been able to show him to Katie. Before she could answer, Katie said, "Because if you are, we can ask God to take care of him. That's what I do."

"So do I," said Clare.

"Well, let's do it," said Katie. She sat up and said, "Please, God, take care of Clare's cat, and let him come home safely. And please help us – I mean, please help Clare not to be afraid of the dark."

Clare opened her mouth to say that she wasn't really afraid of the dark at all. Then she changed her mind, because she didn't want to quarrel with Katie, and because it was nice of Katie to pray about Oliver. They both said "Amen!" and then they both said "Goodnight!" twice to each other. The little light from the lamp was comforting, and Clare could see that Katie's hands had stopped gripping the top of the blue duvet. Then her own eyes began to close and they didn't open again until the morning.

Chapter 6

Clare thought that she and Katie were much better friends after the sleepover. Somehow, Katie didn't seem quite as bossy as before. Or maybe it was just that Clare didn't mind so much. They were learning to understand one another.

There was just one small thing that bothered Clare.

"I don't think Katie really believes we have a cat," she told her mum. "Oliver is so awkward. He's never here when Katie comes. I think she thinks I'm telling fibs about it."

"I wouldn't let it bother you," said Mum,

spooning food into Tommy's mouth. "They'll catch up with each other sooner or later. Cats do wander."

"I know," said Clare. "I've never seen her Thomas either, but I don't think she's making him up. She ought to believe me. Friends should believe one another."

"Quite right," said Mum. "So they should."

That morning, at school, Katie had news about Thomas. "We took him to the vet's," she said at break time. She and Clare had both taken skipping ropes to school that day. Katie skipped three skips, and went on, "I went too."

"Was he ill?" asked Clare.

"No," said Katie. "He needed an injection. Cats do. It's to stop them getting ill."

Clare shuddered. She didn't like injections and felt very sorry for Thomas. "Did he mind?"

"Not really," said Katie. She skipped three more skips and added, "Well, maybe he did. He kind of jumped and spat when the needle went in. But he wasn't bothered before. We put him in his basket, like we do when we're taking him on holiday with us. He probably thought he was going on holiday."

"Poor Thomas!" said Clare. "Was he upset afterwards?"

"Only a bit," said Katie. "We gave him his favourite food for dinner. Chopped liver. Dad said he'll have forgotten all about it in a day or two." She skipped another three skips, stopped and looked at Clare. "Your Oliver ought to have an injection too."

Clare had been going to skip three skips too, but she let the rope fall in front of her. "Oh no! Poor Oliver! It would be awful!"

"Well, he should go," said Katie in her most bossy voice. "Take him soon. Or he might get some awful cat disease."

She skipped six times, and then the bell went for lessons, and they both went in, trailing their skipping ropes behind them.

After school, Clare told Mum and Dad about Thomas and the injection. "Oliver won't have to have one too, will he?" she asked.

Mum and Dad looked at each other. Then Dad said, "I really think perhaps Katie's got a point. Maybe he ought to. It's something we hadn't thought about. But, yes, he should certainly get all the proper jabs. He needs to stay healthy."

"Especially around children," agreed Mum.

Clare wanted to cry. She couldn't bear the thought of someone sticking needles into Oliver. But Dad said very firmly, "It's

Saturday tomorrow so I'll take him to the vet's then."

Clare hoped that Oliver would stay out all Friday night and Saturday morning. But he slept all night on Clare's beanbag and showed every sign of spending the morning with them.

"Trooo?" he said to Clare at breakfast, looking up at her.

"He hopes it's kippers," said Clare, and added sadly, "The poor darling doesn't know what's going to happen to him."

Dad had already borrowed the cat basket from Katie's family. "You needn't come," he told Clare. "Maybe it would be better if you didn't."

But Clare felt she couldn't let Oliver down by staying at home when something so awful was happening to him.

"I'm coming," she said.

Oliver was not like Thomas, thinking that he was going off on holiday in the cat basket. As soon as Dad brought out the basket, he stopped purring and stared at it with narrowed eyes. He licked his lips nervously and his tail twitched from side to side. Dad opened the lid, and Oliver shot across the kitchen towards the cat flap.

"Catch him!" said Dad.

Luckily Clare was standing near the door and was able to catch Oliver. She felt his heart thudding and his whole body trembling. He didn't bite or scratch her, but he made a low grumbling sound deep inside himself. Dad took him from her, popped him into the basket and closed the lid.

Clare felt her eyes fill with tears. She bent down to look at Oliver crouched in the basket, spitting and snarling. She said, "I'm sorry, darling Oliver. It's only so you won't get sick. I'll give you kippers for lunch, I promise."

At the surgery, the vet bent down too and looked at Oliver. "Oh dear! Someone's not pleased. Better stand back when we open the lid."

Dad and the vet both put on thick gloves. Oliver hissed and grumbled in the basket. The vet and Dad hoped he'd calm down, but he wasn't going to. The vet opened the lid.

"Stand well back, Clare!" warned Dad.

There was a yowl and a screech, and a black streak shot from the basket and hurled itself across the room.

"Grab him!" said the vet. "He's terrified."

Dad tried, but Oliver lashed out with sharp claws. A long red streak appeared on Dad's arm above the glove. Oliver scrambled to the top of a filing cabinet and sent a pile of papers fluttering to the floor. He crouched there, spitting and saying horrible things in cat language.

"He's terrified," said the vet again. "Maybe he once had a bad experience at a vet's."

Clare thought that Oliver was having a bad experience right now. Nothing could persuade him to come down from the cabinet. Clare thought she could coax him down, but Dad wouldn't let her try. "I don't want you hurt," he said. "Stay well back."

The vet decided he would have one more try to recapture Oliver. He moved a chair next to the cabinet and climbed onto it, getting ready to grab Oliver with his gloved hands.

Oliver's eyes flashed like fire. He looked

round desperately and noticed that the top of the window was open a little. As the vet reached for him, he dived for it. A plant pot fell from the window sill with a crash. Next moment Oliver squeezed through the narrow space and disappeared.

Chapter 7

Clare arrived home in floods of tears. Mum came anxiously from the kitchen to meet her. "What is it? Whatever's happened? And where's Oliver?"

In between sobs, Clare told her the story. "And now he's gone! He's run away! He might be lost! We might never see him again!"

Mum hugged her. "Now don't worry! The vet's is not that far away from here. He'll find his way home again when he's calmed down."

Dad came in after he had parked the car. "Crazy cat! He went completely bananas!

Never got his injections at all. But Mum's right, Clare. I'm sure he'll turn up, just like a bad penny."

Oliver didn't turn up that day. All day long, Clare kept going to the gate and looking up and down the street for him. There were several cats about, crossing the road or lying asleep on walls or sitting washing themselves. But none of them was Oliver.

"I wish we'd never taken him to the vet," said Clare. "He thought we were going to hurt him. He was so scared."

It was Bank Holiday weekend, and they were off for a couple of days to visit Grandma and Grandpa at their old home. Oliver still hadn't returned when it was time to set off on Sunday morning. Clare was convinced that something dreadful had happened to him.

"Now don't be silly!" said Mum. "There's the cat flap for him to come through when he decides to come home. We'll leave plenty of food and water out for him. He'll probably be here to meet us when we get back."

It was nice to see Grandma and Grandpa again, but all through the two days Clare kept thinking of Oliver. Each night, she prayed very hard that God would take care of him, and that he would be at home when they got back.

But he wasn't. The kitchen was quite empty. The food and water hadn't been touched, and Clare knew that Oliver's favourite cushion hadn't been sat on. He was still missing.

She burst into tears again. Oliver hadn't come home. God hadn't answered her prayers, she thought.

Mum and Dad were busy carrying in the luggage and Tommy, and all the things Tommy needed when he went anywhere. Mum wanted a cup of tea, and Dad wanted to stretch his legs after driving. Tommy wanted to dive into his toy-box and pull out all his favourite toys. Clare just wanted Oliver, but he wasn't there.

Later they sat down to a supper of cold ham and salad and Grandma's home-made pickle. Suddenly, Clare was sure she heard a small sound at the blue door. She held her breath, with her fork in mid-air and pickle on the end of it. Slowly, the cat flap was pushed open and a black shape came through.

Clare dropped the fork, pickle and all, and jumped to her feet. "Oliver!"

It was Oliver, but he looked very different. His black coat was dull and rough, as though he hadn't bothered to wash himself.

His eyes looked dull, too, instead of their usual shiny blue. He was thin and looked as though he hadn't eaten all the time he'd been away.

He paused and looked at them, but seemed so weak and tired that he couldn't even say "Trooo?" to greet them. He walked slowly to the water bowl and lapped from it. Then he went over to his basket, crawled into it, curled himself up and closed his eyes.

"Oh, Mum!" said Clare in horror. "Whatever's happened to him?"

"I'm afraid he's ill," said Mum. "No, don't touch him, Clare. Let him rest. We'd better try and get hold of the vet."

Even though it was a Bank Holiday, the vet kindly agreed to come and see Oliver. He remembered him from Saturday and said he'd been wondering about him. This time, Oliver seemed so ill that he didn't mind the vet looking at him at all. The vet put him gently back into the basket.

"Is he really ill?" asked Clare in a quavering voice.

"Well, the old chap is rather poorly," said the vet. "It seems to me he's eaten something that didn't agree with him at all."

"Poison?" asked Dad.

The vet shrugged. "Maybe. Or some food that had gone bad. He's been very ill, I'd say, but I think he'll recover. I'll give you something for him. Let him drink plenty, and just rest."

"But he'll get better, won't he?" asked Clare.

"I'm sure he will," said the vet. "With care."

All night long, Oliver lay curled asleep in his basket. Clare got up in the night and tiptoed down to look at him. Apart from struggling up to get a drink, he didn't want to move at all.

"I wish I could stay and look after him instead of going to school," said Clare in the morning.

"Nonsense!" said Mum. "I can look after him just as well."

Deep down, Clare still felt that Katie was a bit to blame for what had happened to Oliver. If only she hadn't said that Oliver needed to go to the vet... If only he hadn't been frightened and run away... If only he hadn't picked up the bad food instead of coming home to supper...

Mum said that was not the right way to look at it at all. She said that Katie was in no way to blame. All the same, Clare wasn't as pleased to see Katie as she usually was.

"Oliver is ill," she told Katie at their first break. "We took him to the vet and he ran away and ate something bad. I'm really worried about him."

Her voice sounded wobbly and she thought she might cry again. She expected Katie to say something really bossy, like how to look after a sick animal, or even that she would come round herself and help to care for Oliver. Clare wasn't sure she wanted her there. Oliver was her cat, and she wanted to take care of him when he was ill.

But Katie didn't say anything. When Clare looked at her, she saw that Katie's mouth was down at the corners and that there were tears in her eyes. Katie said, "I'm sorry Oliver's ill. But he'll get better, won't he?" She gulped and went on, "We've lost Thomas. He's been missing for days and days. My brothers think he's been run over."

And then she burst into tears herself.

Chapter 8

Both of them cried for a while, until one of the teachers came and asked what was the matter. She gave them both a hug and told them not to worry too much. Then they went off by themselves to a quiet place in the playground where no one could overhear their conversation.

"Let's pray again," said Katie. So they held hands and spent the rest of the break praying for their cats.

Next morning, Clare expected that Oliver would be quite better and that Thomas would have come home. But Oliver still lay in his basket, thin and weak. He hardly ate anything and didn't really want to get up at all. Clare could see that Mum was worried about him too. And when they got to school, Katie said that Thomas had still not come home. They prayed again at break time, but Clare had lots of questions on her mind.

"I don't understand," she said to Mum that afternoon, when she came home from school and found Oliver still weak and ill in his basket. "God used to answer when I prayed to him... Like when I wanted a friend, and Katie came. And then I wanted a cat, and Oliver came. And then he ran away, and God brought him back again. But now Katie and me are praying and nothing happens. Isn't God listening?"

Mum sat down and put her arm round Clare. "He's always listening. But he doesn't always answer right away. Sometimes he does. But other times there are things he has to work out first. Things we don't understand. Sometimes we have to wait."

Clare told this to Katie next day. Katie seemed to understand. "Yes. I had to wait, when – when –"

Her face had turned pink. "When what?" asked Clare.

"Well, when I prayed for a friend. I didn't really have a special friend before you came. Everybody thought I was too –"

She stopped again. Her cheeks were even pinker.

"Too bossy?" said Clare.

Katie nodded. "I didn't know I was bossy. I didn't know what they meant."

Clare thought of all the big, bossy people

in Katie's family. It was no wonder that Katie had turned out the same. Suddenly, she was glad she had Katie.

"I don't think you're too bossy at all," she said, and she found that she meant it. "And do you know what? I prayed for a friend too. And it was you."

Katie's face broke into a big smile. And then they hugged each other, suddenly feeling much better.

"Oh, I nearly forgot," said Katie. "It's my birthday on Saturday, and we're having a party in the garden, and you're invited."

The week went by. Every morning and afternoon, Clare sat by Oliver, stroking his fur and talking to him. She filled his bowl with fresh water and helped him to drink from it. She carried him out into the garden and encouraged him to walk about and get his strength back. Oliver prowled around a little, to please her. But he was always glad to creep back through the cat flap and go back to his basket once more.

The vet came again. "Try and get him to

eat," he said. "He needs to build up his strength. He's been a very sick cat."

So Clare prepared lots of things she thought Oliver might like: the tastiest cat food, mashed up and warmed a little. She gave him minced up liver and gravy, warm milk, even mashed kippers.

By Friday afternoon, Mum said that she thought Oliver was a little better. That lunch-time, he'd actually got up, lapped some milk, and then eaten a little bit of food.

Then he'd taken himself into the garden, strolled around the flower beds and sat in the sun for a while.

He'd even had a go at washing his fur and getting it back into order. And when Clare came in from school, he looked up at her from his basket, stretched out his forelegs and claws, and yawned. Then he said "Trooo?" in just the way he used to. Clare thought his voice was still a little bit weak.

Clare went down on her knees by the basket. "Oh, Oliver! You're better!"

By morning, Oliver was ready and waiting for his breakfast, and looked almost his old self again. He had given himself a good wash and his coat was neat and shining. While he'd been ill, it had a dull rusty-red tinge, but now the jet-black colour was back. His eyes were bright and shining again. He ate up all his breakfast, gave himself another wash and strolled out through the cat flap.

"I hope he won't go too far," said Clare anxiously.

"He'll go as far as he feels like," said Mum. "He's always been a roamer, and I don't suppose he'll change. Just be glad he's better."

Clare was glad. She saved up the good news to tell Katie when she went to her birthday party that afternoon.

After breakfast, Clare went shopping with Mum and Tommy. They spent a long time choosing a nice card and present for Katie. The card said, "To a very special friend" and the present was a tiny black and white china cat.

They had left Oliver snoozing in the sun on the sitting-room window sill. It seemed to be one of his favourite spots. Walking home up the hill, Clare saw at once that he wasn't there any more. But when they reached the gate they met Oliver, squeezing himself between the bars on his way out of the garden.

"Oh, Oliver," said Clare. "Are you going roaming again?"

Oliver looked at her out of his blue eyes and butted his head against her knees. He avoided Tommy's clutching hands and sniffed at Mum's shopping bag to see if she'd bought kippers today. Then he said "Trooo!" and turned and sauntered away along the pavement. He looked a little thinner than he used to be, but clearly felt quite back to his old self and able to go off on his travels again.

Chapter 9

It was a lovely sunny afternoon. There were lots of people scurrying around in Katie's garden when Clare's dad dropped her off there. Katie's big brothers had put up a large table under the apple tree and it was covered with a bright red plastic cloth. Balloons had been tied in the branches of the apple tree.

There were lots of normal sized ones and one huge one with "Happy Birthday" in big letters on it. Katie's dad had lit a barbecue on the patio and was stoking it up with charcoal. Katie's mum and sisters were running around with folding chairs, paper

plates and cups, plastic cutlery and other things people use at outdoor parties.

Katie herself was pink with excitement. She took Clare inside and showed her all her birthday presents. There were books and cassettes, a yellow canvas rucksack, china animals, a doll's house with furniture, posters and pictures. She was delighted with Clare's present and put it carefully on her bedside table.

Clare told Katie the good news about Oliver. She expected that Katie would be upset, because Thomas still wasn't home. But Katie only said, "I'm glad. That's one half of our prayers answered. I'm sure God will answer the other half soon."

There was a shout from below: "Girls! Food's up!"

There was a delicious smell of barbecued chops and burgers and sausages in the air. They ran downstairs, and were soon tucking into burgers and hot dogs with lashings of fried onions and big dollops of tomato sauce. Crisps and nuts and cheese and crackers were set out on the table. Max hung around, keeping his eye on any stray bits of meat that might fall to the grass.

Clare thought it was a lovely party. Everyone bossed each other around, even Katie on her birthday, but no one seemed to mind. When Katie's mum brought out a huge birthday cake with eight candles, everyone sang "Happy Birthday". Then her brothers and sisters grabbed Katie, one at each arm and leg. They gave her eight bumps on the ground, and one extra to grow on.

"Now you have to cut the cake," said Bridget.

"And we'll take a picture," said Katie's mum.

Katie picked herself up and posed for her birthday picture, ready to blow out the candles on the cake. She had a huge grin on her face.

Then suddenly, the grin disappeared. Katie gave a big jump and screamed. Her mum ran across to her. "Katie! What is it?"

Katie shook her head. She seemed unable to speak. She was staring at the garden gate. Everyone looked in that direction. Squeezing through the bars of the gate and strolling towards them was a black cat with shiny blue eyes, white feet and whiskers and a white bib.

Katie found her voice and she and Clare shrieked at the same time.

"Oliver!" shrieked Clare.

"Thomas!" shrieked Katie.

They both turned to stare at each other, then at the cat, and then at each other again. Katie left her birthday cake and came to stand beside Clare. "It's Thomas!" she said. "He's come home again."

"But it's Oliver," said Clare. "It is. It's my darling Oliver."

Without a care in the world, the cat came over to the girls, looked up at them, said "Trooo?" and then wound himself round both their legs, in and out.

Katie's family were gathering round, welcoming the cat and making a fuss of him. Clare didn't know what to think. It was Oliver, she knew it was. She loved him and knew every whisker of his round furry face. Why was Katie saying it was Thomas?

Unless – She and Katie looked at each other again. The others were looking at one another in a puzzled way too. Then Katie's oldest brother Robert said, "You know what I think? I think this cat's been leading a double life. I think Thomas and Oliver are the same cat."

"Going from one place to the other," said Katie's sister Emily.

"Eating two lots of meals – no wonder he's so fat," said Sam.

"He's thinner than he used to be," said Katie quickly.

"That's because he's been ill," said Clare.

They looked at each other again. Both of them were beginning to realise that it was true. They'd never seen each other's cat when they'd been at each other's house. Cats did roam, they both knew that. It seemed almost certain that their two cats were one and the same.

Oliver/Thomas licked up some sausage

crumbs. Max was watching. Then he sat down and began to wash his paws. He seemed quite unconcerned about the commotion he had caused. Everyone was crowding round, discussing him, but he began to wash his ears and took no notice.

"Where did we get Thomas from – can you remember?"

"I can't really. Fancy him having two homes."

"And two families."

And nearly two lots of injections, thought Clare. She remembered how terrified Oliver had been at the vet's surgery. The thought of the injection he'd had just days before must have been very clear in his mind. Suddenly, she knew that it was true. Thomas was Oliver. Oliver was Thomas. They were one and the same.

She gave a little gulp. One question stayed in her mind. If Oliver and Thomas were the same cat, who did he belong to? Was he her cat or Katie's?

Chapter 10

"I don't know who he belongs to," said Clare that night at bedtime. "Or what to call him."

She glanced tearfully at Oliver/Thomas, who had somehow managed to get home before her from Katie's and was back in his basket.

"Perhaps the best thing," said Mum, "is not to think he belongs to anyone. He comes and goes as he likes. He always has. Nothing has changed. It's just that we didn't know before that he was spending the rest of his time at Katie's."

"But Katie has so many pets," said Clare

sadly. "I only have Oliver. And now he's not really mine. It's not fair."

"You could share him," said Mum.

Clare wasn't sure she wanted to. And maybe Katie wouldn't want to share either. She decided that, once again, she would have to pray about it.

An idea began to come into her mind, but she wasn't quite sure yet. In the meantime, Oliver/Thomas behaved in just the way he always had. Some evenings he turned up at Clare's house, ate an enormous supper and maybe stayed the night. Other times, he was gone all night but appeared for breakfast, or for lunch, or to spend the afternoon. He did just as he fancied, whenever he felt like it.

There was only one difference. Clare knew that when he wasn't at her house, he was at Katie's. She and Katie discussed it at school together. Clare knew that Katie loved the black cat as much as she did. But there seemed to be a little awkwardness between them, because neither of them

knew who Oliver/Thomas really belonged
to.

By the beginning of the next week, Clare knew what she had to do. She told Mum about it at breakfast on Monday morning. "He's really Katie's cat," she said. "We only came here a little while ago, and Katie's been at her house for ages. I know he came here when the other people lived here. But nobody seems to know where he started off. I'm going to tell Katie. I expect he'll still come to see us. But he'll be Katie's cat."

Mum gave her a hug. "If you think that's the right thing to do."

It gave Clare a funny empty feeling to think of giving up Oliver. But she said quite firmly, "I do."

Just the same, it was going to be a hard thing to do. She gulped when she saw Katie coming to meet her across the playground. Katie's cheeks were pink and her eyes shining.

"I've got something to tell you!" she said.

"So have I," said Clare.

Katie didn't seem to hear. She said, "Guess what? We're going to Australia! My gran and grandad live there. For the whole summer, as soon as the others finish their exams! Only it'll be winter there, because it's the other side of the world!"

Clare's head was spinning. She hadn't a clue where Australia was, except that it was where kangaroos came from. Katie was rushing on. "Of course, we won't be able to take the animals. My other grandad is having Max, and the rabbit and hamster are going next door." She paused and looked at Clare. "Then there's Thomas. We talked about it, and we all decided. We want him to stay with you, for good. We want him to be your cat."

Clare felt her mouth fall open. She said, "But – but how will he know? Won't he still keep coming to your house, like he does now?"

"The house will be shut up," said Katie. "There'll be nobody there. Nobody will feed him, or anything. Mum and Dad think he'll give up coming, after a bit." She gulped, and said, "I expect he'll forget us.

But I shan't mind. I'd like him to stay with you. I know you'll love him and look after him."

Clare hardly knew what to say. She'd been prepared to give up Oliver, but now Katie was giving him back to her, for good!

She said, "Oh, I will!" and gave Katie a big hug.

It was a blazing hot Saturday in early August. Mum and Dad and Clare and Tommy had all been raspberry picking. Now Mum and Clare were sitting in the garden. Tommy had fallen asleep in the shade of the garden parasol, and Dad had fallen asleep inside.

A brightly coloured postcard was propped up against the fruit basket on the picnic table. The front of it was divided into four pictures. One had a kangaroo with a baby in its pouch and one had a koala bear. Another had some bright yellow flowers and the last had a very bright blue sea and white beach. On the other side, there was a stamp with a blue budgie on it, and a message which read, "Having a great time. It's a bit cold though. I'm missing you a lot. Hope to see you soon. Love, Katie." There were several kisses and a PS. "Hope Thomas is well." The name Thomas had been scribbled out and "Oliver" written instead.

Clare looked across at Oliver, sprawled out asleep in the sun with his eyes closed. He still wandered a bit, but spent most of his time at their house now. Suddenly she missed Katie very much.

"It's funny it's cold there when it's so hot here," she said.

"Well, Australia's the other side of the world," said Mum. "Run and fetch the globe of the world and I'll show you."

When Clare came back with the globe, Mum pointed out the large pink piece that was Australia. Clare felt a little alarmed. "But it's right on the bottom of the world! Katie won't fall off, will she?"

Mum laughed. "Of course not! The world turns all the time and nobody ever falls off. You miss Katie a lot, don't you?"

Clare nodded. "Do you think she'll be the same when she comes back?"

"I'm sure she will," said Mum.

"Will she be just as bossy?"

"As bossy as ever, I expect."

Clare gave a sigh of relief. When Katie came back, she wanted her to be exactly the same, because that was just the way she liked her.

More exciting books to enjoy in the Read by Myself series...

Mrs Turnip's Treasure
Anne Thorne
When Mrs Turnip asks Adam to look after her 'Treasure' he assumes it is some kind of booty from her great-uncle's pirate ship. But Adam's in for a big surprise!
ISBN 1 85999 052 5
Price £3.50

My Real Rabbit
Geraldine Witcher
At the weekend, Mum said, "I think a boy who is too old for Peter Rabbit might be old enough for a real rabbit. Don't you think so, Mike?"
  Mike stared.
  "Yes please!" Mike couldn't believe it. A real rabbit of his very own!

Mike wants to be grown up, but he discovers that a real rabbit is quite a handful!
ISBN 1 85999 028 2
Price £3.50

Available from your local Christian bookshop